THE EROTIC MODERN LIFE OF MALINALLI THE VAMPIRE

BOOK 1: ACROSS THE POND

Visit the Author's Website at www.vvcastro.com

© 2019 V.Castro

This is a work of fiction. Names, characters, businesses, places, events, locales, and incidents are either the products of the author's imagination or used in a fictitious manner. Any resemblance to actual persons, living or dead, or actual events is purely coincidental.

All rights reserved. No portion of this book may be reproduced in any form without permission from the publisher, except as permitted by U.S. copyright law. For permissions

contact: vvcastro100@gmail.com

Cover by CReya-tive

It's my last night in Dublin before I head to the south coast of Ireland. Even though it's summer, there's always a damp chill in the evening air. What a change from the southern hemisphere of the world, the part I'm most used to. This is exactly why I've decided to cross the pond and explore the Old World.

I'm on my final pub and third glass of white wine with "Big Love" by Fleetwood Mac playing. What a great way to end the evening. The paunchy bartender bellows last call over the din of the bar. People neck whatever they're drinking and shuffle towards the door. Through the thinning herd, a corner booth comes into view.

There he is, sitting with his mates at a table covered in Stella Artois bottles and pint glasses. A box of books, the contents of which all look the same, rests at his feet. Was he peddling them? Did he write them? Doesn't matter. I want him.

We don't find chemistry, it finds us. Perhaps it's a sign that all those long-lost particles blown to bits in the beginning of time have found their way to one another again. Stardust finding itself in another body. Until we reunite with it, our thoughts and desires will burn like meteors, scalding skin, brain, bone, and soul. Fate has decided I'm not going back to my room anytime soon.

The question is, will he notice the only brown girl in the place with the leather jacket, dress too short to bend over, large hoop earrings and lips tinted so red they'd leave a ring around his cock?

The bartender shouts last call again for those of us that remain. I drink the dredges of my wine, waiting for a glance from the stranger in a tweed newsboy cap, jeans, and black

t-shirt that reveals the bottom half of tattoos on both arms. I watch him take the beer bottle into his mouth then lick his lips. Now I'm convinced I want to take him home. Just one last souvenir from my time in Dublin. He's perfect.

Our gaze locks. His eyes are the colour of stormy coastal waters and mine so dark they look nearly black, or so I'm told. Suddenly my thighs are slick—something I notice since I'm wearing nothing underneath my thin jersey dress. The wetness between my legs becomes harder to ignore the longer I stare. His look says, "I'm here," and my body answers, "I'm coming." In this moment I'm a piece of driftwood being pulled to shore by a current I can't control.

I walk over to the table; his friends eye the brazen woman with a hungry look on her face. They are certainly drunk, talking too loud with heavy lidded eyes, but he's not. He *knows* I've come for him.

"Hey fellas." I only greet the others to be polite then turn my attention to the man I'm even more attracted to the closer I get. A stubbly five o'clock shadow covers his face, but not so thick you can't see his cleft chin. I touch his shoulder to let him know my presence is a formal invitation.

"So, can I help you carry those books home?"

A cupid bow mouth curls to a slight smile. He looks at his friends who are too gobsmacked to say anything except stifle their boyish schoolyard giggles. I could give zero fucks what they're thinking, because all I have on my mind is fucking this guy tonight.

"Alright then. I'm not far, my bookstore is just around the corner. My flat is above it."

"If you have no one waiting for you at home, show me the way," I say without looking at anyone but him.

--

We walk into the cool summer night. His arms bristle at the evening air. I don't feel the cold.

I'm curious about this man with the books. "Tell me, why all the books in a box if you own a bookshop?"

He laughs, throwing me a playful glance. Hot damn, is he cute.

"A book signing. I'm a writer. My publisher says something about there being more traffic there, more visibility, blah fucking blah. Sell, sell." We don't walk long before reaching his bookstore.

The shop is dark and narrow in one of those old wonky listed buildings built in the 17th century with exposed wooden beams on the outside. The crooked sign reads, *Horror, Occult and Other Mischief.* Now I *really* like him.

The walls are filled with tightly packed frayed spines from top to bottom. It smells of coffee and musty paper. There's a large tatty sofa facing the door where I throw my leather jacket. He drops the books in the corner along with his hat. His hair is cut right to the scalp. It takes a certain type of man to pull off that kind of haircut, but with those eyes and strong jaw, he can do anything he wants. Only moonlight illuminates the room—it's just enough light to see each other, but dark enough to set the mood. I pull him to me by the waist of his jeans. "So, what do you write?" I ask.

"Horror. I write horror. Shall we go upstairs?"

There's a room in the back with what looks like another sofa and desk. I don't want to wait and make small talk. Being this close to him makes my pussy feel like it's full of bees buzzing around, their movement causing sticky sweet honey to leak from their honeycomb. "Take me back there."

He leads me to an office at the rear of the shop. A desk and plush sofa face each other. A black varnished animal skull with large antlers hangs on the wall, its black hollow eyes overlooking the entire room. I can't get distracted by details or get too personal, even though he piques my interest. I turn my attention back to him. Our mouths meet without any talk or hesitation. His kisses are teasing nibbles, licks, and they tell me everything I need to know about him. I can already feel his hardening cock through his jeans, yet despite his arousal he continues to kiss me like we share a secret sign language using only our mouths. When did someone last try to seduce me? I never give anyone the chance.

I push him onto the sofa while I sit in front of him on the desk. This dress is short enough there is little work hitching it up to expose my wet lips. My dress strap has fallen, unmasking one of my breasts, just enough to tease him.

A little fact about me: I've got a bit of a predilection for voyeurism. I like to see the excitement and anticipation on my lovers' faces. I take them to the edge of desire so once I allow them the pleasure of my body, they hold nothing back, giving me untamed, ravenous sex. Since I'm a free woman now, I live my life without limitations. All the ones who ever told me no or held me back are all dead.

"Stroke your cock," I mutter as I touch myself. Without protest he begins to masturbate as he watches me. I can tell he wants to reach out and touch me by the soft sigh that escapes his perfect mouth and by the pained look in his eyes. His hand glides up and down. Beads of pre-cum call for me to lick it off, wear it like lip gloss, but not yet. The anticipation of getting him alone has me feeling like I'm about to come, but I don't want to do it on my own. He will be rewarded for his patience.

"Get over here now, I want to come in your mouth," I breathlessly command.

He crawls on all fours towards me like a pilgrim at the steps of a church no feet can touch. He remains on his knees so I can rest my thighs on his shoulders. His tongue is soft and it winds around my clit as if he's spelling my name without knowing what it is. Darting between my pussy and ass, the sensations of pleasure spring from me like water trying to escape through a crack in a dam about to burst wide open. I push his head closer to my pussy. He sucks me to the edge of the universe and back with his blue eyes, tongue, and stubble that scratches my thighs. I have to steady myself against the desk as my back arches in ecstasy. It hasn't been long since I last had sex, but I can't remember when I last orgasmed like that. This guy makes me so fucking hot that if he told me leprechauns and pots of gold existed, I'd probably believe him.

Coming once is not enough and his cock is still dripping with something delicious. I push him backwards onto the floor with my stiletto, careful not to hurt him. I can't handle the sight of blood right now.

I lower myself onto him slowly, I want to experience every thick ridge and vein of his cock against my clit. I'm about to ride him like Sissy rides that mechanical bull in *Urban Cowboy*.

He moans once inside of me, as I tighten my grip with my pussy. His hands find their way to my round, fleshy hips. Holding on for dear life, like I'm about to throw him out of a plane, he thrusts from underneath, his entire body tensing each time. I can tell he wants to come. Not before I get my seconds.

"God, woman, who are you?" he groans.

I lean forward, never stopping my grinding, slapping hips from increasing the friction against my clit. My lips are close enough to his ear to whisper, "I'm a horror story."

He grips my ass so hard, if I felt pain it might hurt a little. I start pounding hard against his body as I orgasm on his cock. As my toes curl, joints freeze, and fingers push against the floor, I think I can hear him grunt through my own calls of release. We both get what we came for. I fall onto his chest, satisfied, and close my eyes.

He's the first to speak with his fingertips rubbing my back lightly. "That was unexpected. I was just meeting my mates for a few beers, then going home to write until I fell asleep at the keyboard."

His touch makes me feel nervous, a bit frightened at how good it feels. I raise myself from his body, looking for something to clean my wet legs. He takes off his t-shirt and hands it me. This gesture stuns me. Sexy as hell, a great lover, and kind. Maybe pots of gold do exist.

"Thank you. You sure?"

He nods while looking up at me, a faint smile on his face.

The black skull with enormous antlers catches my eye again. It reminds me of a past life. This thing is like a dark god that just witnessed and blessed our sexual unholy matrimony. The entire room is dark and a bit macabre with spooky little trinkets. He's my kind of guy—with edge, but not so sharp you can cut yourself. Something tells me there are emotions, stories, and thoughts that drop off to dark trenches few see except him. I'm always drawn to those places where not a ray of sunlight dares to shine.

His deep voice breaks my thoughts, "By the way, I'm Colin."

"I'm Malinalli."

He's buttoning his jeans and picking himself up from the floor. "It was a pleasure meeting you tonight. Where are you from? You don't look like you're from Ireland."

I lean against the desk. He moves closer, so close I want to kiss him again.

His voice has an undeniable accent that rolls off his tongue, another little thing that turns me on. "You got those black eyes, beautiful skin the same colour as whisky, although so much more intoxicating." His hands are tracing my neck and breast as he places the fallen strap from my dress back onto my shoulder. I'd be lying if I said it didn't feel good, to be touched liked this. Most of my lovers never get beyond asking my name and not getting an answer.

"You're right. I'm not from here. I'm from Mexico. It's been a life-long dream to explore all of Europe, one country at a time."

The rigours of sex must have worn off, as his body shivers from the cold in this uninsulated old building. He rubs his forearms, then mine. "Aren't you cold?"

I smile to avoid the question. "Got anything to drink?"

He pulls a bottle of whiskey and a t-shirt from a drawer in the desk. I want to leave, but not be in such a rush as to appear rude. At least that's what I tell myself. I like this man. He's into books, a writer of all things, charming, and looks as rugged as the Irish landscape.

My sense of relaxation doesn't last long. With sex out of the way, there's something else, a nagging need crawling beneath my skin. I'm hungry. I need to eat. I knock back the glass of whiskey so fast it goes down my throat in a rush of fire. "Thanks for everything tonight. Good luck with your book."

I start to walk towards the door to retrieve my jacket and find a meal.

"Wait. I don't know anything about you. What just happened was fantastic. How about dinner tomorrow? Meet at the pub?"

Maybe it's how sexy he looks in the moonlight or the grave way he asks, but my mouth says, "I'll think about it," before my brain can tell it to say no.

I stop before I walk out the door. "Hey, can I have one of your books?"

He approaches me with a book and holds it to my chest. His other hand is a feather's touch against my thigh until my ass is in his palm. It takes every ounce of self-control not to devour him with my body and mouth. There is something about his touch that makes me feel so weak. I didn't even know he existed two hours ago. He growls in my ear with his lips barely brushing against my cheek.

"I hope you like blood."

Once again, he reads my mind.

--

I walk the area known for its women of the night. I want to find someone without a pimp and working for herself. Whenever I can help a sister out, I do. Anyone can come on hard times, no one is immune to desperation.

A young woman emerges from the shadows. "Hey sexy, want to walk on the other side of the street for a change? Love your shoes."

She doesn't look strung out or drunk.

"Come closer. Let me see your arms, your eyes. Are you with anyone?"

"No. I'm on my own. My body, my cash. All of it. And I don't use. I smoke pot, do a little coke if it's offered, drink. Who doesn't?"

Hard drugs are a no for me; it's poison to a vampire's system. Otherwise I leave people alone to do whatever they want.

"Honey, I've got cash, but I don't want your body, I want your blood. I'll pay you double and no sex involved. I've even got a topical anaesthetic to numb the pain of my bite."

She furrows her exaggerated drawn on eyebrows. It's obvious she has no idea what I'm talking about. "Triple for the kinky shit."

We wander into a nearby park where we sit on a bench. I wipe numbing cream on her outstretched wrist.

"Close your eyes and listen to music on your phone," I tell her. She shrugs her shoulders and obeys. My feed lasts for ten minutes then I allow the young woman to leave with enough money that she won't have to work for a week. Satiated, my mind wanders back to Colin.

--

I spend the night in my hotel reading his book because I'm finding it difficult to close my eyes and rest. My encounter with Colin has left me on edge. He's left me with so many questions. I want to know what secrets lie behind his imagined worlds. Will they reveal some truth of who he is as a man? The longer I read, the more I long for his touch again. He has talent, wit, and tales I want to be told in front of a fireplace at some lodge in the middle of nowhere. I could spend days fucking him, feeding from him, finding out the things that have shaped him to create horror. I want to sneak up from behind him while he writes, bite his neck, then swivel his chair around so I can hop onto his cock for a ride to ecstasy town over and over again. I guess I have a taste for something more than a one-night stand. If I think about him anymore, my mind might spiral into infatuation. I'm way too old for that shit.

When the book is finished, I stare at the business card I took from his office before leaving, just a token at the time. But having been allowed into his mind after experiencing his luscious body, I'm left feeling like a well that's nearly gone dry, yet begins to fill again upon heavy spring rains. If only he knew of the horror I have lived through in all my years. If someone, anyone, could understand the self-imposed exile I've put myself in, perhaps it would be him. There are only so many promises you can break in one lifetime. Could he, of all people, understand this weird existence of mine? I text him we'll meet him at his place the following night. It's easier to feign eating in someone's home than at a restaurant.

--

He buzzes me through the entrance and I walk up to his first-floor apartment. The door is left ajar, but I knock anyway. The anticipation of seeing Colin again is so great, my belly feels like a cave filled with bats ready to take flight.

"Come in," he shouts. "Sorry, I just need to finish this paragraph. After last night, I can't stop writing. I may never let you leave now."

He sits in a black leather office chair with only the glow of the computer to light the room. The bookshelves that line the walls that are filled with CD's, horror films, and more books. There are so many, the collection spills onto the floor in neat piles. It makes me laugh to myself, smile from a place that I keep in resting bitch face mode. I want time to discuss these beautiful things together. How have I been led to this individual so suited to my tastes? The room smells like laundry detergent and cleaning supplies. How cute that he took the time to make his place decent before my arrival.

"Where's the bed?" I say from behind him. He swivels around and both of his hands reach for my legs and inch their way up the side of my thighs. His touch is like having one of my appendages reattached after being torn away.

He looks into my eyes then scans my body. I've got another mini dress on. This one is leopard print and lace.

"Thanks for texting me. I didn't realize you had my number. Thought you might wander in the shop." He pauses, looks at me. "Why don't you take this off? I like your sexy style, but I want to see you."

I may have lived long enough to be mostly comfortable in my own skin, however, that doesn't take all my insecurities away. Any damage to your body before becoming a vampire remains. His request makes me feel vulnerable, human. If I was capable of blushing, my cheeks would be a shade of scarlet. Sometimes being superwoman is exhausting; sometimes that guard needs to come down.

"I have a scar, stretch marks, it's not pretty. Let's keep this what it is, a fantasy. You're mine and I'm yours."

He leads me to the bedroom and sits at the edge of the bed. There is a serious sincerity in his eyes now. This look has the same effect on me as flowers to other women.

"I don't care what you look like. It's how you feel that matters. What your body did to me last night was mind blowing. Don't hide from me. I'm sure as hell not perfect. I still don't understand why you picked me out of the bar. You look like the kind of woman that could have any man you want."

I'd like to sit and tell him all the little things I adore about him, despite just meeting. I want to discuss his book, take copies of all his books to read tonight, but I've been wet since he placed his hands on my thighs. And now this. The honeycomb inside is crushed and overflowing. My desire for him requires seeing to immediately. But he's right. I've never fucked a flawless human in all my 500 years of sex. Why should I trip about not being perfect?

I pull off my silk chemise. I allow him to look and touch my completely exposed body. He kisses the rough scar that runs vertical on my belly, fingers trace faded stretch marks, large hands grab my wide hips and pull me closer as he sneaks his tongue between my eager labia and moves it around like a finger saying, "Come hither."

He's teasing me, a game of sexual hide and seek with his tongue. I allow my head to roll back and close my eyes. Tiny spiders of pleasure scuttle across my nervous system. Fucking him leaves me helpless to whatever thing wants to carry me away and drain me dry. He explores the rest of me with his hands. I push him backward, so I can now look at his lithe physique. He's not overly muscular, but his body has definition. I smile when I see the small patch of hair on his chest turns into a furry trail that leads below his jeans. A tattoo that matches the skull in his office decorates the skin over his heart. What does it mean? I have to know, but later. Now it's my turn to tease.

My tongue flicks along the shaft of his cock all the way to his anus. I lick his balls, taking them gently in and out of my mouth as my hand continues to stroke his cock. My tongue goes further down to explore his ass like a snake looking for a hiding place. He grips the sheets as the tip of my tongue oscillates around his anus. He's even harder now in my hand. That always does the trick; he's ready for me now. His stiff cock and my engorged clit need to be reunited in perfect unwed bliss. As I move to face him, he grabs me by the waist, tossing me on my back.

"I wish I knew what you were doing to me, woman. I haven't been able to stop thinking about you."

I want to tell him I feel the same, finished his book in one night. I want more words, more touches that leave me feeling human, but I keep quiet.

He thrusts inside of me like a runaway train hitting the side of a mountain and his paw of a hand massages my ass. Volts of pleasure cause the hair on my arms and neck to stand up. His cock is an electric eel bringing me to Bride of Frankenstein life. His rhythm between my legs is incessant, going from a slow strum as smooth as Nile Rodgers's guitar to a vigorous beat that resembles death metal. Our bodies intertwine like we are in love even though I want it to be no more than lust. With every squeeze I feel the wounds around my heart open a little more. His eyes, heavy in their intensity, pry my soul open like a crowbar at a rusty safe.

Our bodies rock in perfect synchronicity. His gaze never leaves my own. As much as I want to bury my head in his shoulder and come, I find myself unable to look away. Part of me wants to tether my heart to this man who is bringing all my demons to the surface. A manhole opened the second I set eyes on him in the pub. It seems I'm not the only one with claws.

He presses his body weight against me as I hold onto his ass with both hands so as not to miss an inch of the thing I crave so much. The harder he thrusts with my bucking hips, the hotter my skin. All my sense of control is slipping through my fingers like severed rope. I can feel my fangs begin to grow. He's bringing out that other side, that dark side I hid so well for centuries. Now I have to look away, try not to let go so easily.

And then he does the unthinkable, my sexual Achilles heel, as if the devil himself whispered my secret. Colin's perfect mouth rimmed with just enough stubble to delight, takes my breast into his mouth, scraping my erect nipple with the edges of his teeth. I come instantly, and he sucks harder, pushes his cock deeper, causing me to come again.

To hide the transformation that's going to happen whether I liked it or not, I push him off my body, so he's on his back again. My lips want to find his cock. Long brown hair hides my changing eyes and growing fangs. His hand gently holds the back of my head with fingers caught in spiderwebs of hair. I want to suck him until he needs an IV to restore his fluids. The entirety of my mouth, down to the back of my throat is filled with Colin. I would take his being inside me for an eternity if it was possible.

Colin's warm sea spray slides without effort down my throat. I continue to suck until his cock is so sensitive he can't stand the feeling of my lips stimulating the head any longer. I jump out of the bed and run to the bathroom. He follows, sensing something wrong.

"Hey Mali, you okay?" I turn my back to the door and hide my face underneath my hair.

"Just…later. I'm fine."

"Please. Did I do something wrong? I'm sorry I didn't warn you before..."

"Go away," I roar.

"I'm coming in. You're scaring me."

I can see in the mirror he's studying my body to see if I'm hurt in some way. His eyes stop. My nails appear bark like and my hands resemble the talons of an owl.

"Mali, your hands, nails."

"Please," I sob. I don't want to attack him or feel anything towards this man except sexual attraction. A bit of fun before I continue my travels.

"Did I hurt you?"

I lift my head towards the mirror, so he can see the real me. "I told you I was a horror."

He stumbles back, still naked.

"What the…what the fuck? This isn't real. Are you fucking with me because of my book? That's not cool."

"No, I'm not. This is me. I'm alive and dead. Calm down. I won't hurt you." My fangs are in full view and the red thread of veins in my eyes pronounced.

"No! Impossible."

I turn around and grab his wrist before he can move away, biting him hard enough to let him know I'm real. His eyes are wide, traveling from my face to his wrist.

"Ouch! Fuck, that hurts! Am I going to be one now? It's real? Those are real fucking teeth." He grabs a hand towel hanging off the radiator.

My heart rate is beginning to slow, breathing stabilizing. It won't be long until I look like myself again. No one has ever transformed me in this way. I've never felt so connected, uninhibited emotionally. But all things come with a price. I was ready to accept this brief glimmer of love was over. "Do you want me to go?"

The white towel is now bright red, like my lipstick that first night. He looks at me in my nakedness with only my waist length hair to cover my breasts.

His blue eyes soften. "No. Don't leave. I've dated worse."

I can't help but chuckle. The taste of his blood lingers on my lips. He tastes like nothing I can quite discern. I want more. When you are deprived for years, one becomes greedy.

As he moves to clean his wound at the sink, he sees me eyeing his wrist. The scent of sex on our bodies and his blood make my mouth water and belly leap.

"Come here," he says in a soft tone. I move close to him so that I'm against his chest. Without thinking, I kiss the skull tattoo and rub my face against his chest hair. He sits on the closed toilet seat and pulls me onto his lap.

"Here." He lifts his wrist to my mouth. "I don't see why you can't have all of me. I knew I was yours from the moment you offered to carry my books."

My worst fear and greatest fantasy floats in his blue eyes that are no longer stormy seas, but cool Caribbean waters that dare me to wade in.

I take his wrist into my mouth and drink deeply. He winces only once then brushes my tangled hair from my face and neck. Lips with the soothing balm that only love can provide kiss my neck. The sticky juice that is Colin's blood invigorates my body. He's swimming through my veins, my heart, my brain. There's no going back the longer I drink. You don't find love when you're looking; it waits in the shadows, stalking you by night, then devouring you whole when your back is turned. I love Colin. When his eyes are heavy, I know it's time to stop.

"Thank you. You didn't have to do that. Why don't we take this party to the other room? Want a beer?"

He kisses my blood- stained lips and pats my bottom. "Hell yes, I want a beer! And a shot of whiskey. And cake."

I roll my eyes, "Cake, really? Why?"

"Yeah, you know when you donate blood you need something sweet after for the blood sugar? You practically drained me! I'd like brownies. I think I still have a few my sister left me the other day."

Any concern I had was gone. "I barely scratched you. I'll be waiting with that beer when you decide to join me." I walk out knowing he's watching my bare ass shake like a perfectly unmoulded jelly.

We sit on his table that seats two and he wolfs down a thick slice brownie.

"I have to ask you a few questions. If that's okay?" This moment was inevitable. I'll try to answer as much as possible, but a woman needs to keep some of her secrets.

"I'm guessing we can only see each other at night?"

I take a swig of beer. "That's totally false. I love the sun. In fact, it's a source of peace and calm for me. I was born a sun worshipper after all—I'm from what is now called Mexico, but I am Nahua by birth. The older vampires operate in the shadows though. I think that's where the myth comes from. Next question."

He's thinking hard as he finishes the last crumbs. "How do you live? Like, do you have a job? How old are you?"

I wouldn't accept this line of questioning from anyone else, but he's not everyone else. I also want to return the favour for giving me his beautiful blood. Perhaps being earnest will prompt him to tell me his life story.

"I deal in antiquities. When the Spanish came to the New World their mind was on nothing but plunder and conquest. Their lust for riches as great as their cruelty. I was given to a very powerful Spaniard as a slave and privy to all the Spanish secrets. Never underestimate the silent woman. You never know what she sees or keeps locked away in her mind for later use. Once I became a vampire I used all my knowledge to hide stolen treasures in various caves around Mexico and South America. As time went on I would visit my secret hordes to sell to collectors or museums. Today I dabble in antiquities from all over. The Internet is a fantastic invention. As far as my age, I became a vampire at thirty, which would make me over 500 years old." He opens his mouth to speak again. I lift my hand. "Later, my love. Bring that hot body of yours closer to me."

We order Indian food for him because he's still hungry, then we curl underneath a duvet to watch *The Lost Boys*. For some reason he's in the mood. It also happens to be one of my all time favourite films. Since I have no spare clothes, he gives me an old Van Halen t-shirt to wear. Not only is his taste permanently in my mouth, his scent is seeping into my skin.

Telling my secret to someone after so many years alone, feels as soft as his twenty- year old t-shirt that I wear with nothing underneath. There is no reason to leave his apartment. I have all that I need. I've moved in without any moving. This is our island within an island.

His idea of breakfast in bed is by far the best sex I've ever experienced and the only thing I want every morning. While still drowsy lying on my side, he greets me from behind with his erect cock, the wet tip sliding between my ass cheeks. As my pussy becomes wetter from his cock entering and exiting, he slides towards my anus. It's stimulated until it pulses like little sea anemone trying to catch prey. His one arm casts around my own, so that his wrist rests on my mouth. His other hand, coated with lube, continues to tease my little puckered hole, sending shockwaves of titillation to my toes.

Once out of my pussy he slides in and out of my ass, pumping to the cadence of a slow ballad like Foreigner's "Waiting for a Girl Like You." His breath on my neck and soft moans are a soothing lullaby. My fingers find my clit as he fucks my ass. I can't remember ever being this wet. His blood is in my mouth and his cock inside my body. There is no part of him that isn't part of me. I want to cry, relinquish my soul to whatever demands the gods have of me because I don't want this moment to ever end. Dreams must exist, because this feels like one in the space of the day that isn't night nor morning. We enter and exit each other's body from the dark morning light until noon.

When I can tell I've weakened him too much from my feeds, I make him all my favourite gringo recipes. We have to do grocery delivery because his kitchen resembles a condiment aisle in a supermarket. If we were in my homeland, it would be traditional food, full of chili, lime, and maize. It's been centuries since a man wrapped his arms around me as I sip on something while tending food over fire. While at the stove, Colin kisses my neck, stokes my ass, then steals my wine. He's a creature of mysterious magic, making me feel desired beyond the quick fix fucks I've grown accustomed to. His allure is so potent, I've forgotten what other blood tastes like or that it even exists.

I read his books in bed while he writes. When he's working, I only sneak to his desk to bring him food or drink. He's writing something new, something with bite and blood and more gore than he ever had in a book before. I consume all of his published books with fervour and then he allows me read all the stories no other eyes have seen. I feel privileged to be a part of something so deeply personal. Before I doze off Colin whispers, "Goodnight Mali, my Nahua muse."

We finally get it in our minds to leave the apartment when his back begins to cramp from being seated for hours on end. The only other time he's left the flat is to check on his only employee at the shop below us. I have to get used to wearing clothes and shoes again. Being nearly naked with Colin somehow feels like my natural state. I'm not even sure how long I've been a tenant in his bed. I'm still paying for a vacant hotel room, but I care little of the cost. This time with Colin is priceless. Finding him, on a tiny little island in an unremarkable pub, is a one in a billion chance. Yes, there are many people out there that would be fun to fuck, but how many of them do we *really* like? He is in my life, whether I like it or not, and the gravity between us is more than theory, it now rules our lives.

The gauzy grey sky gives the city a feeling of sad memory. The dark gloom that settles in the morning remains until the night. Not a speck of sunlight pokes through once. The narrow, cobbled back streets are the most interesting, but he wants to show me the clubs where he'd watch punk bands perform, his childhood neighbourhood, his old school. We sit on the park bench where he had his first kiss. How different we are in our beginnings, our current situations, yet how much of that inner life is the same. We've only met, but I feel like he's been by my side for hundreds of years. Before his parents were born, my soul secretly yearned for this kind of companionship.

I rest my head on his shoulders as we sit on the bench with a light mist of rain falling over us. I close my eyes and want to be my vampire blood entering into his veins, mutating his cells until we are truly the same. I want a shoulder to rest my weary head upon for years to come. Will this stay good long enough for us to get through the entire Netflix catalogue of horror? I dare not fantasize any longer.

"Tell me about the horned skull."

He smiles as he stares into the trees. The few other people that are seated get up to find shelter from the rain. We are now alone.

"Well, I suppose it's what I might look like if you peel back my skin. All the things I feel, think, my regrets, the things that motivate me, look like that. A few years ago, I did a lot of hard drugs. I thought it helped with the creativity, but one bad trip left me hospitalized. I felt like I was going insane. So I stopped. Stopped drinking for a spell too and took a road trip in America. This old guy was selling it in this little junkyard shop off the highway in New Mexico. I bought it straight away and had it shipped to Ireland for an insane amount of money, but I couldn't let it go. When it arrived in Ireland, I had my mate varnish it. It helps remind me to always be honest with myself and others."

Colin's ability to reveal himself to me makes me want to feel him closer. I kiss his lips, unbutton his jeans, slip my hand underneath his boxers, while his navy rain jacket hides my little misdeed. I watch dirty blond eyelashes flutter as droplets of drizzle catch on the edges. Those perfect lips quiver and smile with every stroke of my hand. He leans back, letting the rain splash his face. His body tenses and his jaw clenches, as the pleasure coils in his groin, and he squeezes my thigh. The rain saturates everything, including us, but it could be fire and we wouldn't notice. When he's about to come, I pull his cock out far enough so that I can wring every drop of cum from his cock with my mouth. This park bench now has two special memories.

As we return home, I hear a small basement bar playing funk and disco. It feels like a poor man's

Studio 54 in 2018. The staircase leads to a dangerously overcrowded club, the air humid with suffocating body heat. No one notices or cares. We could all be in the middle of a field under the stars while an angel acts as DJ. I drag him to the dance floor. At least I dance, and he watches or shuffles his feet back and forth as he sips on a beer. He's happy to humour me and give me a twirl, as long as I reward him with a kiss. If I could relive any decades, it would have to be the 70s and 80s. It was a neverending party of pleasure and music. My only best friend was a woman I met in New York City during the 70s. That's another story for another time.

I dance him into a corner when I notice a roped off room in purple velvet and low light. Glancing around to make sure no one is looking, I grab my bottle of wine and pull him inside, pushing him onto the velvet sofa before turning to close the curtains.

My hips sway to the beat of the music. I'm wearing heels and a red wraparound spaghetti strap dress that is very short, just how I like my dresses to be. I keep my eyes on him as I slide a single strap off my shoulder. "I Want Your Love" by Chic is playing. I'm feeling nothing but complete abandon. We might as well be riding on an asteroid in free fall, destined to burn through the atmosphere of a new world. He looks so good tonight in his loose jeans and t-shirt. His stubble is unusually thick today. I want to feel my nipples in his mouth. I want to be driven to hunger and back again since he knows how to do it so effortlessly.

I straddle his knee with one heel on the sofa, grinding my bare pussy above his leg, my dress lifted just enough for him to catch a glimpse of my wet lips. He reaches to touch me and I swat his hands away and turn around to grind against his cock, still dancing. Lost in the rhythm, I kick off my heels to dance the way I danced as a young girl, the way my ancestors danced, conjuring up spirits and magic of the Old World. Perhaps that is the same magic that made me what I am today. I am so very close to finding out.

I whip my hair side to side then bend over to touch the floor, so he has full view of my ass and pussy. Before I make it to the floor, he grabs my thighs, and the stubble that drives me wild brushes against my ass. His tongue laps at my clit, then dances from my labia to my asshole as I hold onto the table in front of the sofa. He moans as he eats me in gulps and slurps like he's gorging on sticky candy. But this is just a an amuse-bouche. I turn around, and see his jeans can barely contain his cock. He reads the look in my eye that says, "Pull those silly jeans down." His fingers unzip his jeans. I love how I don't even have to speak for him to know what I want him to do. You don't need to speak when you want the same thing, when you need the other person inside of you like you need air.

My knees sink into the sofa as I straddle him. My ass and hips still move to the beat, letting the tip of his cock sneak inside of me before it's out again. I bob and plunge deeper onto his cock as the music becomes wilder, while he squeezes both of my nipples into his mouth. Either this man is telekinetic, or the heavens decided to bless me with a seraph to fulfil my every wish. Or is it the devil leading me down the road of ruin, temptation that feels like a downy bed, but is really a coffin? I continue to ride him harder and faster as the music commands and as his grip on my ass tells me to. He's moaning, biting his lips while sweat causes his t-shirt to cling to his chest.

As much as my body wants to extract every ounce of pleasure from his body, I want to cry out, "I love you. I'll love you forever you son of a bitch. What have you done to me?"

I remain quiet and direct my fingers to my clit, creating a hurricane of tension that results in orgasm. Knowing he's made me come, Colin places one hand on the back of my neck as he thrusts his cock as deep as he can manage then comes inside of me. I can't stop trembling as we just stare at each other, our foreheads touching. I don't hear music or people or know if there's anything beyond those heavy purple velvet curtains. He opens his mouth to say something, but before he can get it out, I take a sip of wine and pour it into his mouth with a kiss.

We linger inside of each other, neither of us wanting to disconnect. I want to cling to him. His sweat covers my chest and arms. We kiss for what seems like hours but is really minutes. I touch his face, kiss him once more until my kisses lead to his neck. I bite, drink, take him into my beating heart so that I may live because without his blood pulsing through my veins I would surely die. I can feel him harden again inside of me the longer I drink. It's not a lustful erection but one responding to love. His sweat rolls from the side of his face into my mouth. Blood and sweat is a salty sweet umami that tumbles around my mouth causing my clit to become engorged again. For the first time I understand what the term making love means. It is a vicious lie to think a slave could ever love a master. There have been so many lies surrounding who I was in history. Colin doesn't treat me like a master, but an equal. He asks nothing of me except to be by his side. This makes me love him even more. I move my hips, grinding at a slow and deliberate pace. Small kisses find his mouth again until we both orgasm. His blood is life, his love salvation, and his body the cherry and whipped cream.

Before I can move from his lap, he puts his hand around my waist.

"Wait. One more question. Since a bite doesn't make someone a vampire, what does?"

Suddenly I'm trembling again. Does he want this life with me? I'm broken thing with a fucked-up past and no knowledge of what the future might hold. I fear what happens when the flush of excitement and newness wears off. That moment the touch that feels so exhilarating to start just becomes a sure thing to get off then roll over for sleep because life is more than sex, dancing, and stories. Love is a story, and all stories have an ending at some point.

Against my better judgment I tell him. "I need to ask you if you accept my gift of your own free will. Then I drain your entire body of your blood, but just before death, I give you my blood. Some use the old-fashioned bite method, however, there are those that use blood transfusion. They still need permission, but it's less…romantic."

He's looking at the corner of the room, nodding, touching his puncture wounds on his neck. Only God knows what he's thinking.

"Thank you for telling me. Thank you for texting me and making these last few, I don't know how many days or weeks it's been, but whatever, it's been something special I didn't know existed. Like you." He kisses me tenderly and places my dress straps over my shoulders. I want to forget he's asked me that question because it just leads to overthinking, worry, messy feelings that splash all over me like a wine glass filled to the very top.

--

Old dark streets, football matches blaring from pubs, and greasy chip shops, make me forget I have a flight to catch in the next week. I've spent so much time making love, cooking, reading, and feeding from him, I forgot about my original plan, my desire to see the south of Ireland. My work has been completely neglected. My inbox is a mess. Unlike my historical persona, my work reputation is spotless, until now. Love isn't blind, it's blinding and blotting. Suddenly, the apartment that felt like an expanding universe is just an apartment. He is just a man, a mere fantasy I once had.

Everyone I ever loved in my life is gone. Not everyone wants the gift of near immortality. All of my children refused it; lovers never seemed interested long enough to stay and I've never had many friends. If only I had been given a real choice in the matter, perhaps I would have shunned this life as well. Will I take a chance on love even though the ones closest to us hold the sharpest stakes in their hands? I've got countless splinters inside of me that will never be plucked from my flesh. The overwhelming obsessive love I'm feeling is turning to ugly fear. Ugly like when I wake up without removing my makeup. Black eyeliner and mascara rimmed eyes, mouth smeared with red and patchy irritated skin.

--

Not a damn thing makes sense anymore until he sits down to eat the poppy seed cake I made the day before. I'm on my phone trying to catch up on work. In the most casual manner he blurts out he wants me to meet the family.

"My sister just texted me. Sunday lunch okay? Do you like kids? You mentioned you were a mother once. Anyway, her kids are pretty adorable." And there's the other stiletto dropping. My head hurts with hangover pain even though I wasn't drunk the night before.

"Colin, you know that's asking for trouble."

"Let's just go for dessert. Say you're gluten and lactose intolerant. I promise she'll be making her 'famous' trifle. She always does for special guests. They all keep asking when I'm going to fall in love. Now they'll know they can stop asking."

He's touching my hand from across the table, looking at me with those dreamy blue eyes that feel like a watery grave. I slowly withdraw my hand to my lap.

The word that has savaged my heart for years has escaped his lips. He loves me like I love him. It terrifies me like my existence terrifies humans. I can't breathe. But this is what I wanted—my fantasy could be reality. I just need the balls to take it into my mouth and bite. Once again messy thoughts of consequences, worry, and potential pain if it goes bad, stab the front of my forehead until I feel dizzy. I go to the other room to find my things, toss his t-shirt into the dirty laundry even though I want to keep it.

"Hey, you want to go out? Give me five minutes to…"

"I'm going. You're staying here. I had a plan and I'm sticking to it."

"I thought…"

"You thought what? There is an ocean between us, more than one in fact. I'm not human! I can't give you children or a life or all those things people want before they expire. I don't do family or romance."

He grabs my hands. "I don't need kids, I'm nearly forty. If it was going to happen, it would have happened by now. I'm sick of being in and out of relationships that are nothing but constant ups and downs never knowing what drama is going to crop up next. There's no bullshit with you. There are no expectations with you. You can have my blood for as long as you want, you already have my heart." He wasn't going to let me go easy. Could he sense my real desire to stay?

"Maybe I'm tired of drinking the same blood. Ever thought of that?" I spit these words like venom aimed at his eyes. Now I'm just being cruel. He looks wounded. I want to embrace him, kiss him, tell him I don't mean it. Making love to him this second would make me forget the silly notion that leaving was the right thing to do. I shake my head. No, this is better. I walk out of the door and don't look back.

--

I spend the next few days driving around the Irish countryside in torrential rain or fog as thick as sheep's wool with only short spells of sunshine to crown the beautiful hills. The pubs are all the same, reeking of stale beer and salt and vinegar crisps. No stardust chemistry here. No boxes of books for me to offer to carry. I'm as fucking miserable as the weather.

Before meeting Colin, I had been in Iceland, followed by North Ireland, in countless places with ample opportunity to get laid. Not a single man moved me the way he had. I drive faster to drive these thoughts out of my mind. When I finally reach the edge of the island, the cliffs remind me of home, my real home. The water below, like my emotions would surely drown me if I allowed them to. Colin is the kind of man that haunts you with one look and possesses your body with a single touch. One night is never enough when he puts me under his spell with those sorcerer's eyes. He doesn't even realize he's doing it. Well, maybe he does a little.

Surely in a place as religious as Ireland I could find a priest to exorcise this blooming attachment, these obsessive thoughts of him inside of me. I didn't want to drown in my insatiable lust nor could I ignore it. Some doors once opened are impossible to shut. We all hold the keys to gates of heaven or hell.

I'm exactly 522 years old and promised myself to never be a slave to anyone or anything ever again. I spent years like that under Spanish rule, passed from hand to hand, reviled and called La Malinche. You learn to harden yourself when you're a slave. Eventually, desperation turned to determination. When the opportunity arose to free myself, I did so in a trail of blood. I had to leave my children who were no longer interested in me, and ultimately abandon the only life I knew for the unknown. I chose a selfish, lonely life based on survival. We were all just trying to survive after the Spanish arrived.

But here on this neon green carpet with breathtaking views, there is no peace to be found. Beautiful things are meant to be shared. And the world is changing so fast, who knows how much time any of us have left? When the seas rise and the climate spoils like rotten eggs, there will be nothing left of any of the islands in the world. Colin should be next to me telling me his stories and me telling him mine. I've only given Colin snippets of my tale. I miss the way he would listen and scribble things down like we were living in a knock off version of *Interview With A Vampire*. My treatment of Colin makes me realize what a ruined soul I am. I've seen enough death to know none of us leave this rock unscathed. Probably not, but there is always time for change. It's never too late to have a Scarlet O'Hara moment and take it all back, damn the cost.

I'm supposed to drop my rental car back at the airport today, but I really don't give a fuck. I've caught up on all my emails, profusely apologizing for my unavailability and that's pretty much the extent of what I care about. At some point I will need to find blood. I wander into one last pub. There are only two other people in the place at 4 pm. The village consists of a pub, a minimarket with a post office, and a few stone houses.

An elderly couple tend bar, withered and weathered in a way I will never know, but they have each other in this remote place that could be on another planet. "Islands in the Stream" by Dolly Parton begins to play. They both sing along off key to the chorus, glancing at each other. My heart feels like their skin looks. The old woman touches my hand when I order another drink. My face must have betrayed my heartache.

"You sure dear? You won't find him in there. I'm much older than you so I should know." This stranger's kindness warms my heart. If only she knew my real age. She's right, though. I don't drink the liquor and leave a fifty-pound note. Disregarding speed limits and rain that leaves no visibility on the road, I drive straight to Colin. He's all I want in this world.

I knock on the door of the bookshop that says, "Closed until further notice." I'm feeling desperate. Did I just throw away something so very precious because I'm too chickenshit to face my fears? I've made a lot of mistakes in my life, but this might be the worst if he doesn't answer. If he doesn't open the door to the shop, I will break the door that leads to his apartment. Then I see a silhouette approaching though the glass on the door. He answers, and I can't help but notice a duffel bag sitting next to the entrance.

He doesn't say anything, only pulls me to his chest and kisses me. I'm on the verge of tears. "I'm sorry. For everything. I'm an asshole for leaving like that. What's with the bag? Are you leaving?" His arms envelop my small frame.

His blue eyes shine like a beacon. "I wasn't going to let you go that easily. I know there is a lot more to your life than you're telling me and that's okay. We have time. I was about to try to catch you before you left Ireland. I didn't care how long it would take, as long as I found you." I don't speak, only kiss him hard. His lips melt me to pliable caramel every time.

"Where are we going?" he asks me through kisses.

I grab his bag. "We're going to London. Got a bit of unfinished business with someone. And I hope you packed your laptop. I think you might find a story there."

Printed in Poland
by Amazon Fulfillment
Poland Sp. z o.o., Wrocław